For Dilys and Sheila

Thanks to Nathan Sanders,
seamstress Emily,
and Cricket, the wonder cat

This paperback first published in 2014 by Andersen Press Ltd.
First published in Great Britain in 2013 by Andersen Press Ltd.,
20 Vauxhall Bridge Road, London SW1V 2SA.
Published in Australia by Random House Australia Pty.,
Level 3, 100 Pacific Highway, North Sydney, NSW 2060.

Copyright © 2013 by David Wiesner
Published by special arrangement with Clarion Books,
an imprint of Houghton Mifflin Harcourt Publishing Company,
and Rights People, London.

10 9 8 7 6 5 4 3 2 1

British Library Cataloguing in Publication Data available.

ISBN 978 1 78344 116 7

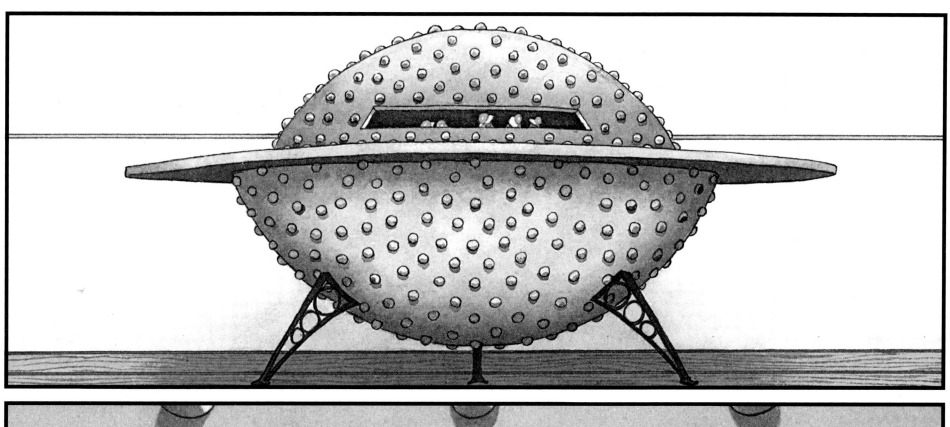

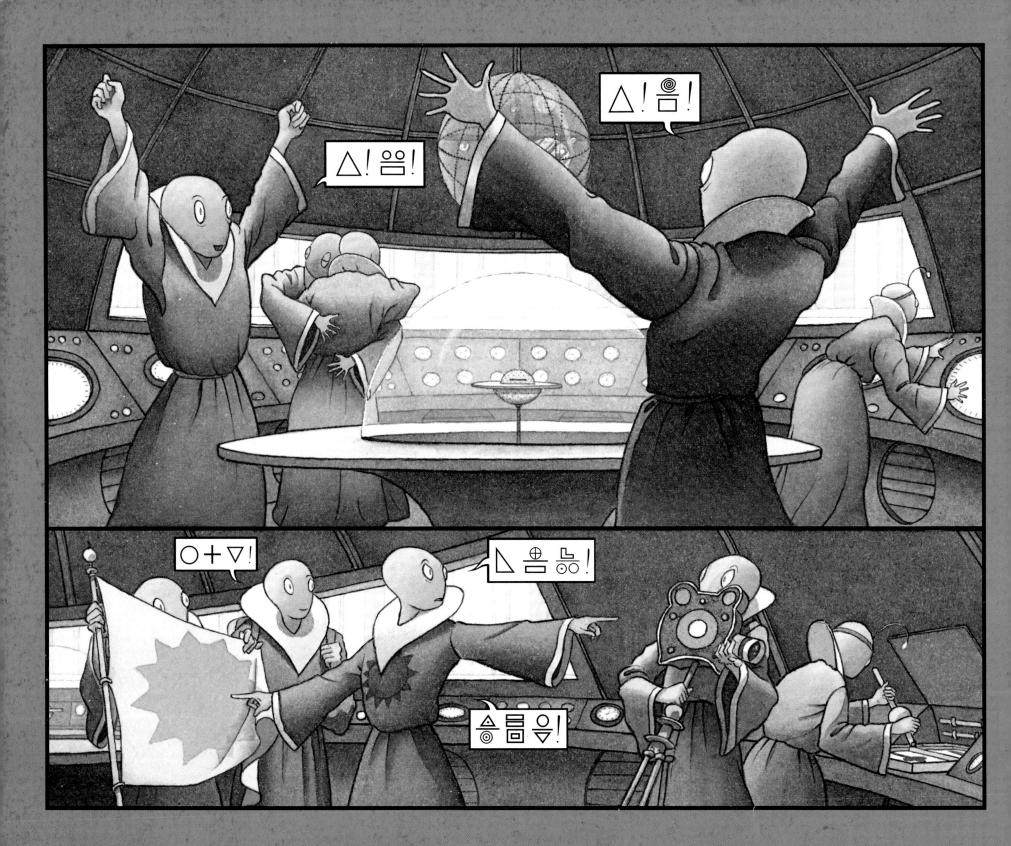

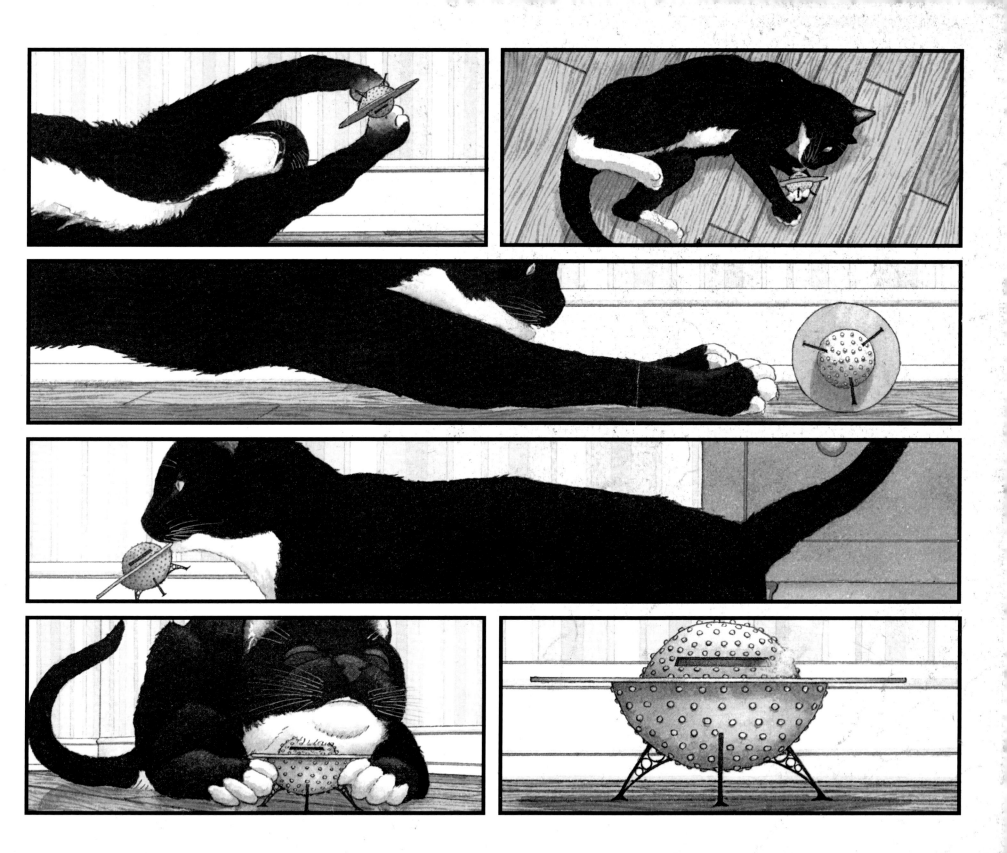

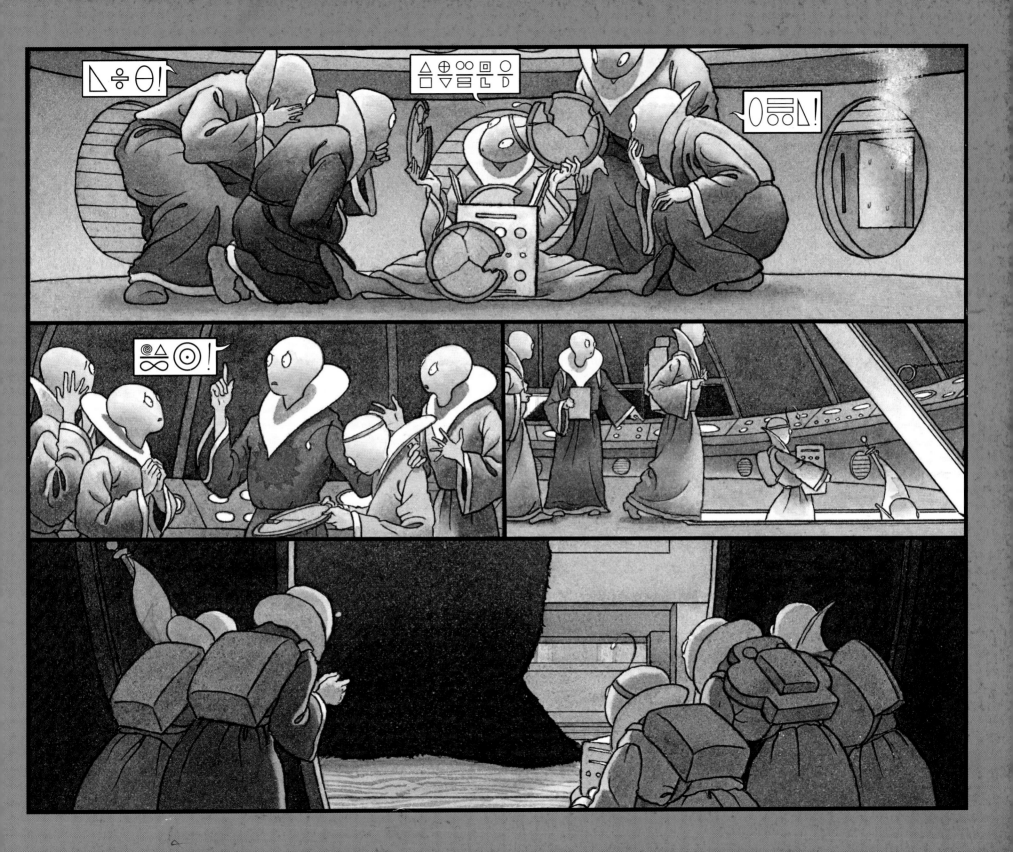

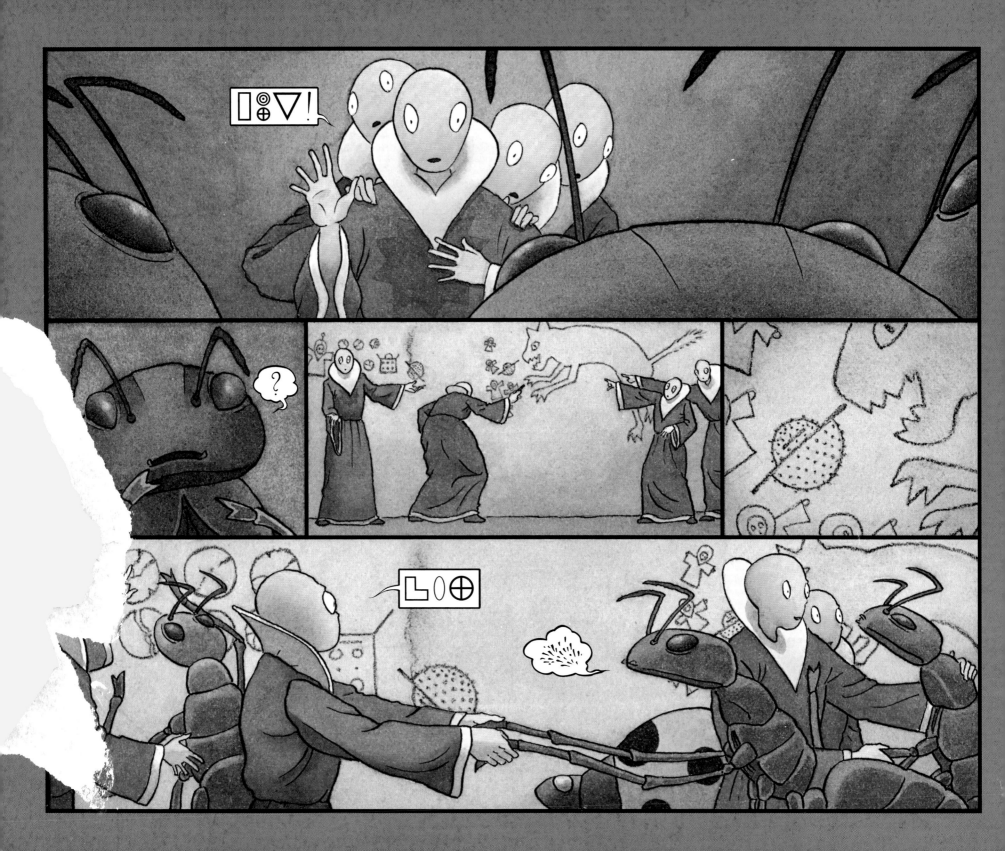

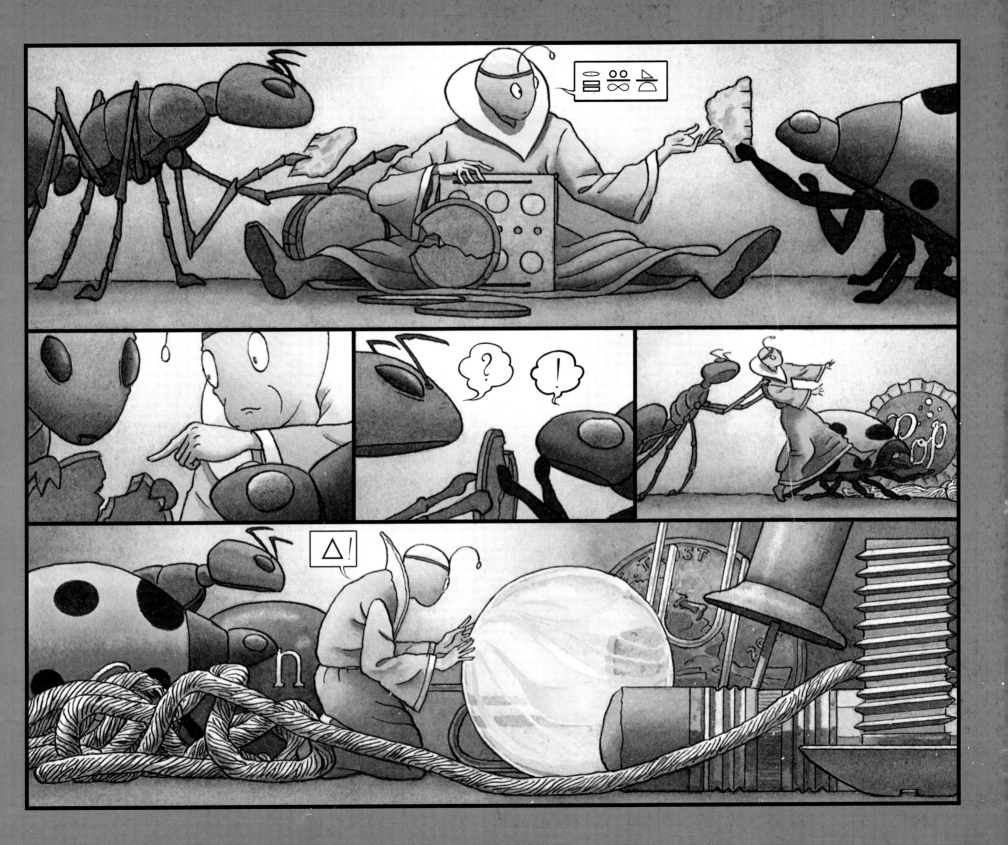

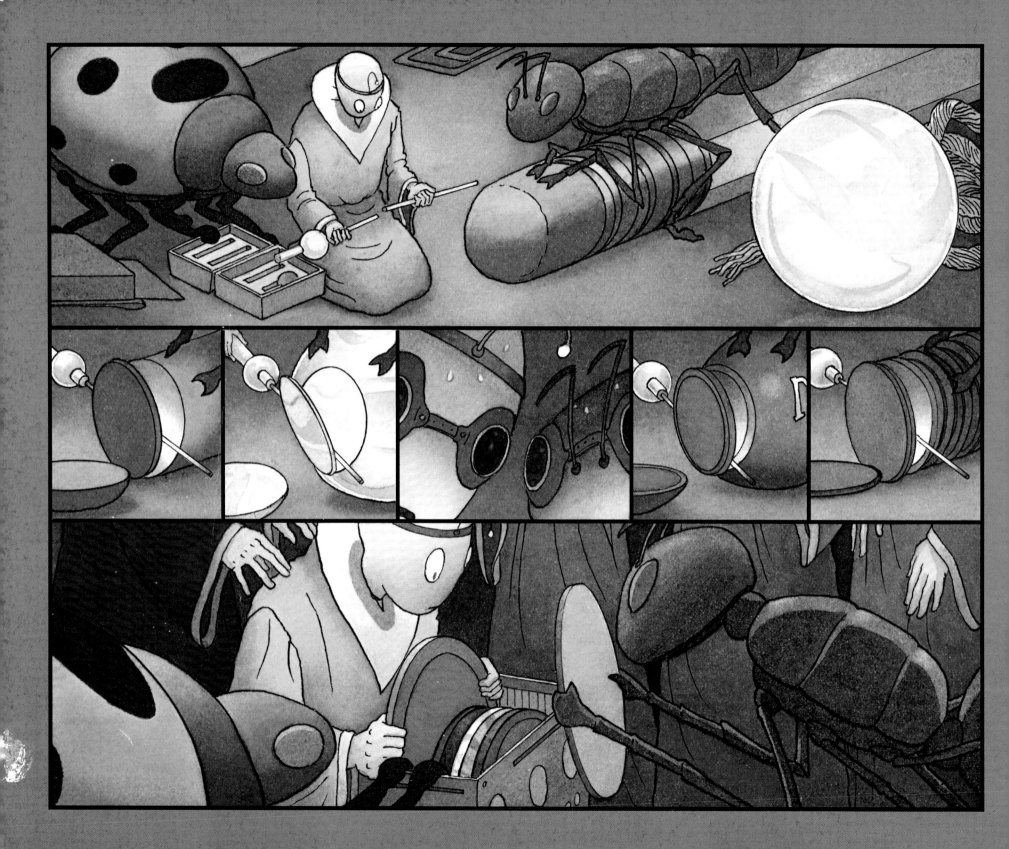

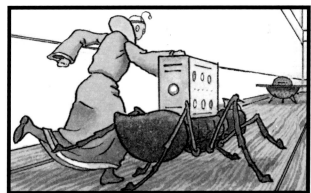

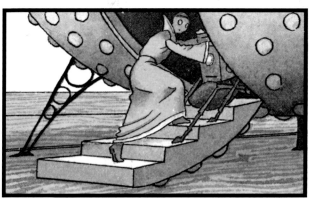

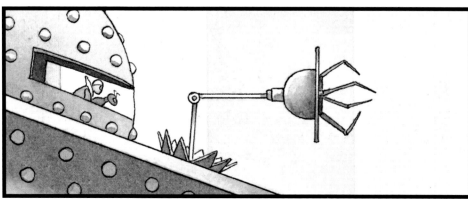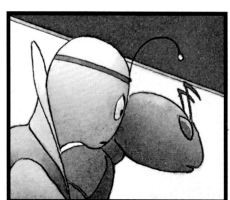

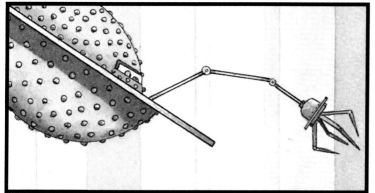

MROWW!